CONFESSIONS OF A MADMAN

Book 2

Author's Note

This story is a work of fiction. Any places, events or characters mentioned are products of the author's imagination or used fictitiously. Any similarity to real events, characters or places is unintentional.

Front cover photo thanks to Pexels

Chapters

Chapter 1

As Jade and Amanda were bringing the rest of the team up to date on everything they knew, the chief constable walked into the room. He started talking, interrupting Jade, to inform them he had spoken to the various stations which had one of these cases, and while they were prepared to cooperate, they each wanted one of their own men involved. This was a good thing he told the crowd, because they would have knowledge of the area and people involved.

As he turned to leave, he threw over his shoulder, "I want daily updates, in fact I want them every morning, every afternoon and every evening. Is that clear?" And he looked at Jade.

As everyone held their breath, knowing this was ridiculous and impractical, Jade replied, "No sir, it isn't. Are you saying you want me to stop investigating or interviewing people so I can be at the station to bring you up-to-date?" She put her hands on her hips in a confrontational manner as she said this.

"Jade be quiet and get on with your work. I will update the chief constable." Brendan stepped in to avoid things getting even worse.

As he said this, he virtually marched his boss out of the room and into the office. Everyone heard raised voices and knew that poor Brendan had a very hard time of it running interference for them and putting up with an incompetent boss.

When he came back out he told Jade not to worry about it, it was sorted. How it was sorted out, or what it had cost Brendan, was not mentioned. He had simply used another form of blackmail, pointing out that if Jade had to spend all day keeping the chief up-to-date she wouldn't be working the case, and if the press got hold of that it would be very detrimental to the chief, and Brendan wouldn't like that. (This last was as far from the truth as could be. He would be delighted if someone outside their station recognised what an imbecile they had to put up with.) Knowing which buttons to press, made Brendan's life a little easier, and as he had suspected, his boss backed down immediately when faced with the possibility of bad publicity. Only saying that Brendan was to tell him when anything significant happened.

The rest of the day was spent organising documents and discussing with each officer what their caseload was like and how soon they could be free. Everyone wanted to work on this case because it was the most exciting investigation they had seen in their whole careers, but few of them could. The majority needed to keep working on the everyday things they had to cover. Jade was using caseload and a few other excuses to try and only fill her team out with men she was the most happy to work with, and these included Davies and Thompson.

She took them into her office to have a word with them alone, while Amanda carried on searching the Internet for more information.

"Guys, you and I both know that if there is a punch-up neither Amanda nor I are likely to win, despite our training. I know you are not here to do physical jobs, but there might be times when I ask you to come with us as sort of bodyguards. I do not want you to be offended, this does not reflect your work and is not the limit of your capabilities, but we might need you. The other side of that coin is that people will often unload more easily to a woman than a man, so Amanda and I might do the interviewing while you stand or sit in the car, just in case something happens. I do not want you to feel upset about this, and if it causes you problems please tell me now and I will find a couple of other officers to do it."

Although neither man relished the task, they saw Jade's point, both about the disadvantages of the woman and the advantages, and agreed that providing it was an occasional thing, they would have no problems with it.

"I want one or both of you to liaise with the other stations, obviously Amanda could liaise with their own, but I prefer to have one person doing it all. That way it is easier to keep tabs on what point we are at and what information we are giving out. Amanda will need to go home and get some clothes and I will go with her so we can talk to the guy who confessed to her. I want one of the two of you to come with us and when were not here the other one of you will be in charge. I don't mind which of you two comes, and which stays. We can see closer to the time if one of you is working on something or not, it's just a heads up that within the next few days that will happen. We will have to go and talk to the other people as well. One of them is a convicted criminal, actually two of them are convicted criminals and are in prison, although one of them is reckoned to be a basket case and is in the psychiatric wing. I have a lot to sort out and do and tomorrow I will assign everyone jobs.

I want to have a quick word with all the guys together so let's go and we can do that now."

Jade was aware her speech had been a little messy, but this had all happened so suddenly she hadn't had time to prepare, and rather that rehearse a speech for ages, she thought it better to let the facts be known and get on with the job.

They walked into the main room Jade where asked everyone to use their spare time to look for anything similar to this kidnapping and murder on the Internet and also to talk to any other officers they knew from other stations to see if they could get more information, or more cooperation.

By that point it was evening and time to head home. There was no point in becoming worn out at the beginning of an investigation. It could be a long time before this went anywhere and undoubtedly there would be late evenings and all-nighters before the end.

It was tempting to stop and grab a bite to eat in the same place as the previous two evenings on the way home, but Jade and Amanda decided it was time to start eating properly again. They hadn't opened the fridge for days so weren't sure what was still good or not. For that reason they went to the supermarket to grab a few things that would make a tasty but quick dinner. That evening they had pasta with ready-made sauce and a glass of wine each. The following day they would need to think more carefully and plan some meals. They both agreed to spend their day off stocking the freezer with home-made meals such as lasagne, casseroles, soap and anything else that could be lifted out in the morning to heat up in the evening.

Chapter 2

As they prepared and ate dinner, the women discussed how to organize their team.

"I think the first thing is to set some people on finding out if they can uncover more cases," Jade said. "Then others to try and find a connection between all the victims."

"Or a connection between all the deaths. I have been thinking, and maybe the people we call victims, because they were forced to kill, are casual. Maybe the deaths are the thing." Before Jade could point out the obvious, that the man couldn't be sure which person his victim would chose, Amanda hastened to explain her thinking. "What if he wanted to ruin a business or a family? It wouldn't matter which person was killed, as long as he reached his goal. I know it is a long shot, but we can't afford to ignore the possibility."

"I think you are right. I hadn't thought of that angle. What else do we need people to do?" Jade asked. "I know there are the interviews with the victims… I have just had an idea," and here she paused to collect her thoughts. "Normally the dead person would be referred to as the victim, but in this case we are calling the people who were kidnapped victims. We need to think of what to call the bodies. Something that is elegant. Body or dead person is too cold."

“So is cadaver, or corpse,” Amanda added.

“How about victim 1 for the kidnapped person and victim 2 for the body? Not ideal, but all I can think of.”

Amanda agreed it would do, unless one of the men could come up with something else tomorrow. (They couldn’t, so those titles stuck.) this was the first time there had been two victims in a crime, at least two in the sense that one victim caused another to become a victim as well.

“Anyway, what I wanted to say is this; “I know there are the interviews with the victims 1, but we also need to get our guys to interview the policemen who took the original statements to see if there is anything else they didn’t write down, and get their impressions. I would like to do the interviews with victims 1, and I am sure you would too. Davies or Thompson will come too because a man’s point of view could be useful.”

“We should get someone to speak to a lawyer to see about a self-defence plea for victims 1,” added Amanda. “I know self-defence allows you to use reasonable force to defend yourself or another, but how far this extends is another matter. If we could offer victims 1 this plea, it might bring in more people willing to testify.”

“Good thinking,” said her friend. “We also need interviews with friends, family and co-workers of both victims 1 and 2. We need a connection.”

“That is probably enough to start with and will keep the men busy for some time. When are we going to my house?” Amanda asked.

“I thought the day after tomorrow. What do you think?”

“Sounds good,” said Amanda. “I will organise to speak to the man who confessed to me then,” and she suited actions to words by picking up the phone to call her boss immediately. Jade stopped her by pointing out it was late. They had been discussing this case for hours and time had got away from them. She could call from work the following day, but for now they needed to unwind so that once they went to bed, they would sleep and not spend hours going over the case in their heads. A light-hearted film did the trick, and they woke up invigorated and ready to go the next day.

Jade called a meeting first thing in the morning and met the officers from the other stations, the ones who had also had one of the odd confessions or a murder that seemed to fit the profile. She said she wanted to talk to them in the office later, but for now she outlined what needed done and asked for questions or suggestions. There were many questions, which she answered easily, but no suggestions. The only question she struggled with was how many of these cases did she think there were. She had no idea and told the group that, along with her belief that they still hadn’t come across his first attempt. She felt sure that it would not have worked out so perfectly. Very few criminals started out perfectly, and this guy was probably no different, so if they could find a case where something went wrong, that might be the clue they needed.

Added to their thoughts of the previous night was also the idea that a person already convicted of murder might be another victim1, and that was something else that needed looking into. She was unable to assign specific tasks to a person due to the fact they all had existing cases they needed to wind up before they could dedicate all their time to this. Therefore she listed things to do in order of importance and asked whoever was free to do them.

When they had finished the meeting and interviewed the officers who had dealt with the other, similar cases, Amanda phoned her boss while Jade sat back and thought.

Ideally she would have preferred to have more cases so she could compare notes about each one, but that also meant more people had died, which was not a good thing. This was so unlike any other case anyone had ever had, she had no point of reference for dealing with it. The enormity of what she had undertaken hit her now as it hadn't done before.

She had always relied on what she believed was her gift, but if her friend was right, she had no special powers, and that left her uncertain about her abilities. She held dear knows how many lives in her hands, and the longer she took to close this case, the more people who could be ruined one way or another. It was a scary thought.

Before she had time to get depressed, her friend spoke to her, and she remembered they were in this together. Amanda was great, and extremely competent, so any deficiencies she, Jade had, her friend would make up for. This brightened her up, knowing her back was covered by a truly great policewoman. Then too, her male colleagues had voted for her to lead this, so they must feel she was up to the challenge. She would show them all they weren't wrong.

Thus, with added vigour, she turned to find out what Amanda wanted to tell her.

"We have an appointment to see Thomas Brothers, my victim 1, tomorrow at ten thirty. We will go straight to see my boss afterwards, and that gives us time in the afternoon to go to my house so I can collect some things. My boss wants to speak to us and to meet you. John is nice, you will like him," Amanda said.

"You call him John?"

"Yes, we all do. He says it makes for a better working environment, but he never lets us forget he is the boss.

That was certainly different to Jade's own experience. Maybe she should transfer after this. It would be nice not to have to fight every day because her boss wanted her to quit and was a total imbecile too.

The day passed in a blaze of activity that concluded nothing but laid the groundwork for much, at least that idea was what appeased both woman.

Chapter 3

Davies was busy trying to finish his own workload, so it was Philip Thompson who accompanied the women to Landing Point, Amanda's hometown the next day.

When they got to the mental institute and asked for Thomas Brothers they were directed to what was laughingly called 'the lounge'. This was a large room with plastic chairs and tables and a lot of people sitting around half dressed in a sort of comatose state.

Never having been in an insane asylum before the three officers felt somewhat uncomfortable. They were told they had to leave anything sharp with the guards before entering, and this even included items such as pens. This was in case the inmates took them and used them to hurt themselves or others. They were informed the patients sat about in a room together, free to move about, but there would be people watching so if they had any problems, help would be at hand.

As they walked into the room the attendant who was accompanying them told them to ignore everyone and ignore anything that was said to them because ninety-nine percent of it wasn't true.
They entered the room with their heads down and were taken straight to Amanda's victim 1. They asked if they could speak to him somewhere in a private room but

were told this wasn't possible and they had to make do with talking to him at a table in the room with everyone else. He looked wary as he saw Amanda approached but as she was the one who caused him to be locked in here, this was hardly a surprise.

The man nearest to Thomas Brothers was yelling at the invisible alien seated at his table to leave him alone, and a lady close by was asking for her vodka that someone had stolen in a very loud voice. It was impossible to be heard in there, never mind have an intelligent conversation. Amanda didn't even try and the trio walked away without saying anything, eyebrows raised.

"We need to speak to Thomas Brothers alone. Can you take him to a room please? And don't tell me again we have to do it here. This is a police investigation," Jade tried to keep annoyance out of her voice, but they had specifically made an appointment to speak to him and she had expected everything would be ready for them.

Jade, Amanda and Philip Thompson watched in astonishment as two burly attendants went and helped Thomas Brothers to his feet, supporting him as they left the room. Obviously they had understood the tone brooked no excuses this time.

"I don't think he's going to be much use. He looks like they have him so full of drugs he won't even know his own name," said Philip. Jade's blood started to boil, but it was Amanda who questioned the attendants when they all went into Thomas Brother's room.

"Is this where you expect us to interrogate him? Are you telling me there is no office we can use?" Amanda asked somewhat dryly.

"The patients aren't allowed in the offices," one of the thug-like attendants said.

"Mr Brothers do you remember me?" Amanda asked, sure he did from the distrust on his face the first time he saw her.

There was no sign he had even heard.

Amanda squatted before him where he sat on his bed. "Mr Brothers. Mr Brothers! Can you hear me?"

"Mr Brothers do you remember me?" enunciating each word slowly and carefully.

There was no reaction at all. The man just sat staring straight ahead. Perhaps the wary look on his face wasn't because he remembered the officer, but his normal expression.

"What have you given him?" Jade demanded of the two attendants still present.

“We didn't give him nothing.”

Frustrated and unsure if these men were being deliberately obtuse or they were just devoid of any brains, Jade tried again, “The word is anything, never mind. What has he been given?”

“We don't do that. It's nothing to do with us.”

Jade demanded to speak to their boss and was told she would have to come back later in the week. At that she said she wouldn't be returning. She would be speaking to the boss immediately. She sent the men to go and get whoever was in charge, adding that if they weren’t back within five minutes they would be going to jail for obstruction of justice. Philip raised his eyebrows at that last comment but said nothing until they were alone in the room. “You know you can do that,” he said, not as a question.

“I know, and I know I let my temper get away from me, but we made an appointment specifically for this.”

Amanda meanwhile was on her mobile and she heard her say, “John the people in the mental home are being obstructive and they have doped Thomas Brothers so much he can’t speak. Do you have any authority to make them stop giving him the medicine so he is capable of understanding what we say and answering questions?” Silence followed while John obviously replied and then

Amanda said, “We did ask to speak to whoever is in charge but they are not keen on letting us do that.” Another pause was followed by, “Okay thank you sir,” and she hung up the phone.

“John is going to call here right away and tell them that Mr Brothers is part of an ongoing investigation and failure to produce him in a fit way to be interrogated, will be an obstruction of justice, as you said Jade.” This provoked a few smiles all round. However, it wasn't a coincidence; Jade had not said it off the top of her head. They were obstructing the investigation by this silly behaviour, and she got the feeling it was deliberate. She couldn’t for the life of her see what they had to gain by this, but then people often acted in a strange way with no apparent reason.

It was about ten minutes later when someone came into the room with a very surly expression and said he was in charge. “No one told me had to be off his medication,” he protested huffily.

“Actually we did, you are just too stupid to have understood it, or you deliberately mis-understood. We have yet to decide which it is. If we tell you we want to interview the man, it is obvious he must be able to understand us and to reply. Otherwise there can be no interview.' Jade paused a moment, and as the man opened his mouth to speak she continued, “Are you his accomplice? Is that why you don't want us to get information from him? Are you afraid of something he might tell us?"

The man's face turned red. "How dare you. I am not anyone's accomplice and I resent the accusation."

"It certainly looks like you are," Philip added his weight to the conversation to stop the guy looking such daggers at Jade.

"We will be back after lunch. You will have him in a fit state to totally understand and reply to any questions we have. Can you do that by two o'clock?"

"I… We… I need to speak to a doctor. Dr Schwartz will know," the man stuttered.

"Get one here right now," Amanda ordered.

A doctor was summonsed, and he said it would take about six hours for everything to be out of the man's system, so four o'clock, or five o'clock in the afternoon was the earliest they could hope for a functioning human being.

"If I told you it had to be done by two o'clock otherwise you would be in jail, what would you say?" Amanda asked, having carefully worded it as a hypothetical question and not a threat.

'I would say it can't be done, but we might manage three o'clock. If we give him a lot of liquids in may flush everything out of his system earlier." The doctor looked terrified.

Jade and Amanda were concentrating on being able to speak to the victim so much they didn't really notice the doctor's overreaction, but Philip did. He wondered what the doctor had to hide that made him so terrified of the police.

"We will be here at three o'clock and he," pointing to Thomas Brothers, "will be ready to be interrogated then. Both of you," pointing to the director and doctor, "will also be here. I don't care if you shift ends or you have appointments. You will be here. One of two things will happen at three o'clock; either we will interrogate Mr Thomas Brothers or you will both be held responsible, and I think by now you have understood what that means." Jade turned and the three police officers left the room. They marched through the building and out to the car park where they all heaved a sigh of relief.

The atmosphere in the place was terrible and the feeling of something awful in the air had touched each in a different way. This was when Philip pointed out the doctor's reaction and suggested they look into him. It was easy for Amanda to look up his records, and she intended to do just that while she was in her station, but as they were in the car about to pull out a nurse walked out of the building and Amanda had an idea. She got Jade to stop the car and jumped out. She went over to the nurse who seemed terrified, quickly looking all around as if to see if anyone was watching, and after only a few seconds Amanda came back to the car.

“We have an appointment to meet her in five minutes just up the road. Go out the gate and turn right, at the crossroads turn left and a couple of miles up the road is a forest. Take the turnoff into the forest and there is a clearing there with benches. She will talk to us there.”

Her two companions wanted to know what Amanda had said.

'I asked about how they treated the patients and if she had any information she could give me about Dr Schwartz. At that she got panicked and said, ‘N*ot here not here*,’ and then told me about this place in the forest.”

“Do you think she will come?” Philip asked

“She’ll come. I told her if she didn’t, we would come back in an official capacity to talk to her.”

“Well done,” said Jade as they went to the meeting place.

In the end they had to wait about fifteen minutes, by which time they began to have serious doubts that the nurse would show up at all. When the car pulled in they could see another person in the passenger seat, a man. Once they were all out of their cars and sitting at one of the benches in the clearing, the nurse said she had gone to get her friend, Freddie, a male nurse, because what she had to say involved him too. She also told the group that she was only prepared to give them the information if they promised that no one would ever know it had come from her and Freddie.

They agreed to this, explaining that they were only interested in Dr Schwartz, the director of the clinic and how the place was run. The nurse seemed a little intimidated at facing so many law enforcement officers, but she took a deep breath and started.

“It was about three months ago. Freddie and I were dealing with one of Dr Schwartz’s patients and when we went in to see him we found him in a coma. The first thing we did, after calling for help, was check his chart to see what medicine he had been given.” She stopped here to explain that every single pill or injection must be listed on the chart because what a patient had taken influenced the treatment it was safe to give. When she was happy they understood the vital importance of this life and death chart, she continued.

“It was another doctor, Dr Harris who arrived first. He started doing all the normal procedures, after he had asked us about medicine, but just as he was about to give the patient an injection Dr Schwartz dashed in and stopped him. He said he couldn't give that injection because the patient that had some Nefuron, a powerful sedative that is still experimental and no one knows what side-effects it has. Dr Harris said it wasn't on the chart, which he snatched from my hands to check, and sure enough it wasn't there. Dr Schwartz said he had been called away before he had time to write up the chart but no one believed him. It is just something you do not do, and he should have found one of us and told us to add it to the chart immediately if that was the case. Besides which, it is not approved yet. It was a gross oversight and Dr Schwartz's actions should have got him fired, if not struck off as a doctor. This wasn't the first time something like that had happened. I sneaked a look at his record one time and he had been let go from another place for exactly the same thing. He had given a patient medication without writing it down. This was probably because it was medication he shouldn't have been giving, but it keeps people, like the ones we have in the clinic, so docile they don't cause any problems. It's handy for Dr Schwartz but bad for the patients. We all hate it."

"Is that why you sneaked a look at his medical records?" Amanda asked.

"No. It was because he caught me alone in a room and cornered me. He threw me on the bed but I managed to scream a couple of times before he put his hand over my mouth and tried to rape me. Freddie heard my scream and came in. Dr Schwartz left without doing me any harm, except giving me a terrible fright, but he made both Freddie's and my lives as miserable as possible after that. Before we had a chance to do anything, he reported me coming on to him and getting violent when he refused. By the time I'd stopped being hysterical and Freddie had given me his jacket, because my own top had been ripped so badly it wasn't covering what it should, and we went into the director's office, Dr Schwartz had got his own version in first. Even though Freddie stated that when he had entered Dr Schwartz was holding me down with his hand over my mouth and trying to force himself on me, the director believed the doctor and not us, and he too tried to make our lives miserable. We reported them both to the medical board and are waiting for the outcome of that, but in the meantime our lives are extremely hard in there and if anyone knows we told you this, they will become worse."

Freddie put his arm round the nurse, who had said her name was Julie, and comforted her because reliving the experience had upset her a lot.

"If you have reported it, that report will be around somewhere. Maybe we can find that and do something about it without anyone knowing you told us,' Philip said, feeling terribly sorry for Julie and Freddie.

That brightened Julie up and she had more she wanted to tell us. "I have no proof, but I believe the patients are all kept over medicated so life is easy for the director, Dr

Schwartz and maybe one or two other doctors. Dr Harris left after that incident and as far as I know he didn't report anything. It seems like most of the staff are part of the thing and all think it's great that they have so little work, but we both really care about the patients and hate to see it. When we can, we take away some of their medication, and some of them are really nice when they're not so sedated."

That was all the information she had for them, but it was enough for each officer to hope that maybe they could do something about that and help these two people while getting enough information to make the dear doctor and director more cooperative in their case.

Time to visit Amanda's station, so that was the next stop. Jade and Philip initially addressed the boss as chief constable, but he immediately said, "Call me John, everyone else does."

They explained everything to him from the beginning, including how they had stumbled upon this by accident. Unlike Jade's boss, this man thought they had done an incredible job and it was very clever of them to put the pieces together and do something about it. He also said he totally understood why Jade's boss had put her in charge of the case but Philip interrupted explaining that he hadn't done it willingly. He told the man that the whole station had to rebel in order for Jade to get the merit that she deserved. John asked Philip if he had an idea about

why this was so, and Philip replied simply that not only was the boss an absolute bungling idiot, but he was also a chauvinist and misogynist.
“'I hear great things about your station. You have wonderful numbers,” meaning the number of cases they solved, John said.

“Yes Sir, er… John, but that is due to Brendan not the chief constable.” Jade explained how Brendan stepped in every chance he could to do the best job possible and to allow the other officers to do their best work too. “We would do a lot better work if Brendan was in charge and we would be of more use to the community as well,” Jade told him.

“Have you ever thought of getting up a petition? If all of you signed it asking for the chief constable to be removed due to incompetence, and you cite various incidents, then I think something would be done., But it would need to be all of you,' emphasizing the ‘all’.

“Tell-tale Tommy won't sign it.,” Philip said. Then realising that this man had no idea who he meant, he explained the simpering idiot that Tommy was. Saying that he might be even more stupid than the boss and that he loved telling tales and tried to get ahead by stepping on people's toes and doing no work at all. Brendan had asked for Tommy to be fired on numerous occasions, but the boss always said he wasn't that bad and Tommy stayed, even after he caused a member of the public to be killed.

“I seem to remember hearing somewhere that your boss has his nephew working under him. That wouldn't be him by any chance would it?” John asked.

Neither Jade nor Philip had had any idea that the boss’s nephew was in the station but they said they would find out because if Tommy tell-tale Tommy were indeed family, that would explain a lot.

“Anyway, back to the case. What have you got? Where are you at and what do you need from me?” John asked.

Amanda explained the problems they had had that morning and what they had found out from Julie and Freddie. John immediately called one of the others into his office and asked them to find out about a report with the medical authority about Dr Schwartz and any past history of his being in trouble, the director of the institute too.

Amanda had intended going home at lunchtime to get some things, having had to reorganise her plans after the abortive morning, and make sure there was no food that needed to be got rid of. It was one thing preparing to be away for a week, but totally different if it could turn into a few months. However, when John said he would like to take them all to lunch, they felt they had to agree and did so with pleasure. Before they left the station, John phoned the mental institution again and told the director that he would be coming with the officers at three o'clock and if Mr Brothers was not ready, and in a state to answer questions, then somebody would be in serious trouble. He hung up without waiting for a reply.

"If we had that sort of help just think how much we could accomplish," Philip said to Jade who nodded. John had heard and was worried by what they had told him about their boss. He said nothing to the officers, but he did intend to look into the matter. It was no use if the person at the head of a station was putting obstacles in their way instead of removing them.

They had a nice lunch and enjoyed each other's company. John told Jade and Philip that if they wanted to transfer, he would be delighted to have them there and they both said that that certainly appealed, but they would solve this case first and then think about it.

Amanda was resigned to not collecting her things until after they had interviewed Mr Brothers, so before going back to the clinic they dropped into the station to see what news there was of Dr Schwartz.

The officer had found the attempted rape report and the cover-up accusation, just as Julie had said. They also had Dr Schwartz's past indiscretion, the one Julie had mentioned, but there was also another one before that as well. The director had also had some problems because families of patients had complained to the medical authorities that their loved ones were being given so many drugs it was frying their brains, but nothing had been done about it.

Chapter 4

Now the police were ready for war and went back to the clinic, armed with information. I think one of you should come with me and we will speak to the director and Dr Schwartz while the other two speak to Mr Brothers. Who is going to come with me he asked, looking at Jade and giving her her due, as the person in charge of the case. Before she could reply Philip answered that he would accompany John because he thought the two girls were the best ones to interview the victim.
That decided, they entered the building and it wasn't long before they got their war. Mr Brothers was in better shape, but they were still expected to interview or interrogate him in his bedroom, which was no use. John used his authority to commander one of the offices and they all moved in there. Then John and Philip took the director into his office and made him call Dr Schwartz.

They sat down and as agreed beforehand Amanda started talking to Thomas Brothers, but when it became clear he was reluctant to give out any information Amanda backed off and Jade took over.

She started by telling him the man that she believed him and was there to help him if he would help her. This certainly got his interest.

“Why should I believe you after what she did to me?” He asked somewhat belligerently, pointing to the woman he had first confided in.

“I think you need to remember that what you got you in here was not her,” indicating her friend, “but the fact that you killed someone. If you weren’t here you would be in jail, and I don’t think that is a better place, do you?”

“But I only did it because he made me. That must count for something. And I gave myself up. I always heard the police went easier on people if they confessed but yet here I am. He could still be out there terrorising my family and nobody is doing anything about it because nobody believes me.”

“We will check on your family and make sure they're all right and local forces will also keep an eye on them. We do believe you, but surely as an intelligent person you can see that your story is somewhat incredible. Would you have believed it if someone told it to you?” This stopped man short, because the truth was that he wouldn't have, and he knew this himself.

“All right, but what's different now? Why do you believe me now?”

“Someone else came forward and told us the same story and it is too strange to be a coincidence. We are investigating it and we are also trying to find out if we could get your charge reduced from murder to self-defence, but for us to do anything, you going to have to help us. Just because you are in here doesn't mean you can go free. If you leave here, you will face a murder trial as things stand. The other man I told you about went insane, literally, so he can't be of any use. What you think? Do you want to help us and at the same time help yourself or not?" Jade had deliberately left out the other cases. She needed this man to think he was the only one who could give them ammunition to help save himself.

Amanda weighed in for the first time at this point, "If you want to have any chance of getting out of here, this is your only option. I would take her offer up and co-operate."

"All right, what do you want to know?"

"Anything you can tell us. I know the guy was masked but was he tall, short, thin, fat? What about his voice, did he have an accent? Are you certain it was a man?" The answer to all those questions was that it was a man about the same height as victim 1, so around five foot ten or eleven, and the man spoke slowly and quietly in a threatening way, but his words were distinctive. The guy couldn't tell them anything else about his kidnapper.

"Where were you when he kidnapped you?"

“I had just left work to go…” a slight hesitation here, “and get some lunch. I felt something in my back and a voice told me it was a gun and to keep walking.

He made me turn into an alley and there was a car parked there. He got me to climb into the boot and as I was doing that he hit me on the head. He then drove me somewhere remote, no idea where, it was just a field.”

Amanda stepped in. “Was he behind you all the time from when you left work? Never beside you? Or did you by any chance see his reflection in a window as you passed?”

“No, I saw nothing. He told me to keep looking ahead and to look down at the ground. Obviously I've thought about it a lot and I'm sure he wasn't wearing a mask on the street because he would have looked odd and I don’t remember people staring, but I couldn't see him.”

“Do you remember what date and time this happened?” she asked.

The guy remembered it very well was able to tell them with certainty.

Amanda was making a note to check the area he had said this happened to see if there were any CCTV cameras that could pick them up and help identify the kidnapper.

They got footage, but it was pretty useless as the kidnapper didn't show his face. They knew only he was average height and average build, something their victim 1 had already told them. This just confirmed it.

“I know you were probably so frightened you didn't take in much, but you may have registered things that you aren't aware of knowing. Would you let us hypnotise you to see if there's anything in your subconscious that can help?” Jade asked.
The man wasn't sure about that and wanted time to think about it.

They asked some more questions and left with the agreement that he would think about the hypnotism and also what happened that day. Anything more he wanted to tell them he was to ask an orderly to get in touch with them. They would leave word that they were to be contacted immediately. He asked them to keep his family safe in exchange for this, and they promised to check on his family and keep an eye on them. Both officers assured him it was unlikely the man would do anything to his family. He had got what he wanted and would have moved on to another victim they insisted.

Once they were outside Amanda complemented Jade for thinking of the hypnotism idea. It may turn up nothing, but it was certainly a very valid idea to try. I knew you were the best person to lead this investigation and ideas like that that prove I was right. Jade was delighted with this complement and the respect of a fellow officer.

They waited for Philip and John outside and it was a long time before the men joined them. John suggested they hold off on any exchange of information until they were sitting with a cup of coffee in front of them, and he drove to the nearest café.

The first thing Amanda said to her boss was to ask him to keep an eye on the guy's family although they honestly believed the kidnapper wouldn't touch them.

The girls recounted the interview and John agreed to set up a hypnotist if the man agreed to do that. Like Amanda, he was impressed with the idea and said so.

"Jade is quite a girl. She conned us with a fake car lift so we would accept her," Philip said to Jade's astonishment.

"Yes, we figured it out, but only a lot later," he added with a smile at Jade. "We were impressed with your ingenuity, anyway, so don't worry. You made your point."
Naturally John and Amanda wanted to hear the details, so Jade told them. John laughed.

Then it was the boy's turn, and they went over every detail of their interrogations.
It turns out Julie was right, and more or less the whole place was in agreement to keep the patients so sedated

they required nothing and were no bother. Anyone who cooperated got extra time off, and staff who didn't, had to work longer hours. Dr Schwartz was in charge of getting the medication without leaving a record, so he couldn't be fired as that would ruin everything.
John had called the medical board while they were there and he and Philip had reported everything to them. Someone was on the way to deal with the staff, and John had asked officers to come and arrest both men. He had left word that Mr Brother's was not to be sedated again as they may need to speak to him at any given time.
Jade asked him to also tell whoever was now in charge that the man was to be allowed to speak to her or Amanda any time he wanted, and immediately. John did this on his mobile and they all settled down to enjoy their coffee.

When they separated, as a parting shot, John told Jade to call him anytime she wanted, even if it was only to talk over an idea. She thanked him and felt a huge burden had been lifted. This offer meant she was no longer alone at the top; a lonely place to be, as showing any weakness or doubts was not really an option.

They made a trip to Amanda's place next so she could get whatever she needed, Jade checked the fridge while Amanda packed. Philip loaded all the meat in her freezer into a cooler bag as well and soon they were headed back home.

They stopped for diner along the way and both Jade and Amanda decided they liked Philip even more as time passed. He was honest, giving credit where it was due, and feeling no resentment if someone thought of something he had missed.

Likewise, jade complimented him on noticing the doctor's reaction which led to the clinic being run better, at least they hoped so.

Philip was also good looking, but Jade had never really noticed this. Amanda did, thinking he looked Nordic. Tall and blond with blue eyes, he really was a hunk, to use an old-fashioned expression. She wanted to find a way to ask her friend if he had a girlfriend, but without Jade thinking she was interested. She wasn't really sure she was, and anyway, this was no time for romance. They had a killer to catch, but no harm in admiring him from afar.

Chapter 5

It was late by the time they got back that night and it had been an exhausting day. Once again they had made no forward progress, which was exasperating and frustrating. This did not help the mood in the car during the journey, but all three slept well that night from sheer mental and physical fatigue.

The day after their journey was spent catching up on what had happened, or rather hadn't happened during their absence. They also had to make out a report and speak to Brendan to tell him everything that had transpired.

Amanda did some checking and discovered Tell-tale Tommy was in fact the boss's nephew. She did this in a fit of pique after she was hauled in front of the chief constable because he had been informed, (he wouldn't say who by), that she had bought a coffee machine for her and Jade. This, he felt, was unreasonable to 'his boys', even though she had spent her own money on it, and therefore it was none of his business.

"Your little spy left out one important fact – your 'boys' got a machine too," she replied a little smugly as this fact had obviously been left out only to create problems for her. "If your 'boys' do not like having a new machine, I am happy to take it back. I will ask them," and she opened the door and yelled, "The boss says you are unhappy about the coffee machines. Do you want me to remove yours?"

Shouts of, "Don't you dare," and "just try it," were the answer.

"So, what would you like me to do?"

"Get out!" was the only answer, and she did, furious.

That was when she checked and found the relationship.

She walked up to Tommy and whispered in his ear, "The next time you think of telling tales on me or anyone here, think of your tongue. If you do that again I will cut it out. And if you think you can tell your uncle of this threat, just know my own boss is my father and will do anything to protect me, and I mean anything. He will even hold you down while I do it. How far will your uncle go for you? If I were you, I would be afraid of the dark. One night, when you least expect it, I will have my revenge, and it will be brutal, really brutal. The last guy I beat up died after about thirty minutes, but I learnt from that and can now prolong your suffering for hours. You messed with the wrong person this time. Now I think about it. You told tales on my friend too, so I think I will take a finger for each time. How many were there?" it was apparent Tommy was too scared to reply, so Amanda told him not to worry she would ask Jade.

She turned and stood on a chair at that point.

“Hey guys,” she waited until she had everyone’s attention. “Little tell-tale Tommy here ran to his uncle while I was away and told him I had got a coffee machine which only Jade and I could use and you were all annoyed about this coffee machine.” There were some startled stares, so she repeated herself. “Yes, you heard me right. Didn’t Tommy tell you? Your boss is his uncle. That is why he is so protected. Maybe we should all take Tommy for a drink after work when it is dark, *away from the office*.”

Her inference was clear, even to dim-witted Tommy, who shrank into a corner amid cheers of ‘Yes, let’s.’

Amanda approached Tommy. “Want to have a drink with us all later on. I know a great bar down a little alley.”

Tommy ran from the room.

“I think one of us should wait for Tommy near his car when he leaves and walk him to his car. I am sure if we take that sort of care of him, things will change around here. He is terrified and it should take little to totally intimidate him. we don’t need to do anything, he just needs to think we will.”

She got a loud cheer from the ‘boys’ and a few of them volunteered to do it that night. Others said they would do it the following night, and Amanda wondered how long Tommy would last before he asked to be transferred. It took three days before he called in sick, and another week before he put in for a transfer. One of the men had put a bug on Tommy's coat and they were even able to turn up at a restaurant where he was having dinner with his mother and father.

Phrases like, "Please don't worry about your son, we all keep a close eye on him," had his doting parents exclaiming about how kind his colleagues were, while each word made Tommy even more afraid. They contrived to leave at the same time and suggested accompanying Tommy home to keep him safe. "We catch bad guys, but sometimes they get off and want revenge. We don't want anything to happen to Tommy," they told his mother. He spent the night at his parent's house to avoid them taking him home alone, and never went back to the office.

Amanda explained to anyone who mentioned it that she behaved that way because she knew her boss had her back, and after this case she didn't have to put up with the chief constable, something the others would continue to have to deal with. She was in a different position to the rest of them. She could afford to annoy the boss, just because he wasn't her boss.

The men had been trying to close their own cases as quickly as possible, and had even put in extra hours to do this. Working on a serial killer case, even though technically this was a serial kidnapper, was every policeman's dream. Especially without the hassle of being responsible for anything. However, progress was so slow and clues non-existent, and morale had started to drop drastically and quickly. Amanda's little trick gave a much-needed boost to everyone, and although it wasn't related to the case, the thought of not having to deal with tell-tale Tommy any more made everyone feel good.

Not only did you need to watch your back with him, but anyone who worked with Tommy knew they were in danger. During one case they had been trying to arrest a drug dealer and buyer. They wanted the dealer to tell them who his contact was. The dealer had pulled out a gun. Tommy shot the guy before anyone could stop him and without giving a warning. One of his colleagues had been standing right beside the man when this happened. Then Tommy turned round and shot the buyer who was unarmed. At least, this was the theory. In practice he had shot an innocent passer-by, grazing his partner's leg as he did this. The boss had covered this up quite successfully, but not only did this cause hatred and worry over Tommy, it told everyone in the station, that the boss was not on their side and would not protect their lives.
It was a big deal to be rid of the danger that was Tommy. However, while this helped morale a little, they still worried that the case was going nowhere.

They didn't blame Jade, for each of them knew this was an unprecedented investigation. The more they worked on it, the more they themselves found out the difficulties inherent in searching for a mad confession. At some point in their careers most of them have had heard some

sort of confession that was blatantly untrue, and just as they hadn't given it any consideration, so they found their colleagues in other stations hadn't either with their own confessions.
For this reason they were mainly concentrating on looking for convicted killers who had claimed they had been kidnapped and forced to kill, for they felt this was the best hope. As yet, nothing worthwhile had turned up. So it was that as they were winding down to go home that day, Michael one of the officers, took a call. It was from a colleague in another station who had just had a confession that matched theirs, and the man who confessed was still there.

'*Did that they want to go*?' Michael replied they would be there in about half an hour and to wait.

He rushed into Jade and Amanda's makeshift office and told them.

"Get a car Michael. We will tell Brendan and be right with you," said Jade. They dropped everything and simply telling Brendan they had a confession and the man was still in custody, they dashed off, keen to hear what the man had to say.

Michael had had the foresight to ask if the guy was incoherent, in a panic or had totally lost the plot. His colleague, David, had replied that the man was cool, calm and collected.

As they drove there the excitement in the car was palpable. If this really was one of their serial kidnapper's victims, a cool, calm and collected witness was exactly what they needed.

Every case had one pivotal thing that changed everything and let them close the case. If that element wasn't there, the case generally remained unsolved. This could be that point.
Each person had to keep reminding themselves that the confession may be false, or unrelated, and it might not help their investigation, but still they couldn't help but feel hope.

Chapter 6

Their excitement didn't last long, because when they arrived, they were met with bad news of a sort.

"The guy, Jones, has asked for his lawyer and refuses to answer any questions until he gets here," David informed the group.

"With your permission we would like to go in and try to talk to him. Perhaps because we only wish to discuss the kidnapper, and not his crimes, he will agree," Jade said. David agreed to this, and Jade and Amanda went in alone, Michael and David watching and listening on the other side of the two-way mirror. Everyone was conscious that the lawyer could arrive at any minute, and generally they ruined interviews, not always in their clients' best interests. They needed to find out as much as possible before that happened.

Jade started by telling Jones they weren't interested in his crimes, but only in trying to catch the kidnapper and asked if he would talk to them about that right away because time was of the essence. Jones pondered this in silence, then agreed.

When they asked him to recount everything that had happened, it was pretty much an exact copy of Mr Brother's account. He had been kidnapped while walking along the street. Someone had come up behind him, forced him into the boot of a car and taken him to a deserted field. He was then given the ultimatum, along with photographs and information about his family, and offered details of how to deal with the body.

“Mr Jones, the man you killed, I am only asking about him in relation to the kidnapper, so any question I ask, is about that. All right?” Jade queried.

“Ask, and will see,” was the cautious reply.

Jade asked if the man felt the kidnapper pushed him to choose a certain person rather than another, and explained she wanted to find out if the kidnapper wanted a specific person dead or was it genuinely ‘just anybody’, as it appeared.

Mr Jones took this question seriously and thought about it for a while before replying. “I don't know, it is possible he wanted Jake dead. It is public knowledge what I thought about the man.”

Jade looked at Amanda and saw the same incomprehension on her friends face that she felt.

“Mr Jones, it might be public knowledge, but we don't know what you're talking about. Could you explain?” Amanda asked

He did.

Six years earlier, his wife, his pregnant wife, had been abducted and raped to death. The police got semen from her and were able to get DNA and find the perpetrator. He was arrested and during the interrogation, which Mr Jones had been allowed to watch, the guy had often said the same thing, '*that woman was asking for it*', but as Mr Jones pointed, out the man, who he called a beast, didn't use the word '*woman'* he used a rude, derogatory term.
Anyway, he, Jones, was told it was an open and shut case because the evidence proved beyond any doubt that Jake had done it and he had admitted it during the interrogation.

When they went to court however, things were very different. The DNA evidence had been lost by the police. During the interrogation there was no mention on the tape of a name, so when the guy said 'that woman' was asking for it, there was no way to prove what woman he was talking about, and he insisted it was his girlfriend he meant. This was a grave mistake on the policeman's part. Then, while was being held in custody, someone had beaten the accused up, so anything he said after that was considered invalid because it was a forced confession.
There was also the matter of evidence being contaminated. Apparently the policeman in charge of the investigation had put something in his pocket, without putting it in an evidence bag and therefore anything it was found to contain was not proof that Jake had

anything to do with it. It could have come from the policeman's pocket, or at that point, as Jake's lawyer pointed out, there was so much police incompetence he wouldn't be surprised if they had planted evidence as well. The guy walked out of court free.

"When he was declared not guilty in court I was so distraught and furious with the police I stood up and yelled, '*This isn't finished. If the police don't get you, I will'*."

There were two policemen on my case, one nice and one horrible. It was the horrible one who made all the mistakes. The nice one came to me after the court case and suggested I bring a civil suit against the other policeman for negligence, and he said he would testify. I desperately wanted someone to pay and looked into that, but the nice partner disappeared, so I had no case really, and let it drop.

Jade and Amanda were shocked and scandalised by the level of incompetence shown in the handling of this case. "Who was the officer in charge of the case, the horrible one" asked Amanda.

"Detective Hardwick," he replied.

"Detective Benedict Hardwick?" Asked Jade.

The reply was affirmative.

Amanda seemed to have caught on to Jade's thinking and looked a question at her friend. Jade nodded and they both sighed. That was something they would have to look at later, but for now they wanted to get as much information as they could before the lawyer arrived.

“Mr Jones, I want you to think very hard and I understand it may seem repetitive considering what you've just told us, but this is very important; “Did you choose who died, or did the kidnapper push you into that choice? Did he say anything like, ‘you can have revenge’. or ‘you might feel better afterwards’ or anything that would lead you to one person rather than another?'

Again Mr Jones took the question seriously and thought hard, “No he just said choose someone you know, and it must be someone you know, and kill them.”

“So if you had had another person you hated, you could have chosen them and he wouldn't have known. So you are saying he couldn't be sure you would kill that guy? Sorry to repeat myself but this is very important,” Jade insisted.

“That's right, and I wasn't even sure when I left there that that was what I was going to do. Naturally, it was what I wanted to do, but I wasn't sure if I could find a way to do it, so I did think about other possibilities but discarded them. To be honest, as long as you do not hold this against me," and once he was sure they wouldn't, "I even considered killing that Detective Hardwick because I thought he was just as responsible, but thought I would bring down the wrath of every policeman in the country."

Jade secretly thought, 'It is a pity you didn't', but for obvious reasons she could not express this sentiment.

Changing the subject, "You said he told you how to dispose of the body, was this a suggestion or an instruction?" Amanda asked.

"It was a suggestion. He suggested a way and said, '*naturally you can do it any way you want, but this way you should get away with it. It's up to you'*." A slight hesitation here made the two policewomen wait to see if there was more, and there was.

"Actually that was a phrase he used a lot; '*it's up to you'*. He used it when he told me to choose between my family and someone else, he used it when you told me I was free to choose anyone as long as I knew them, and he used it about the body. I think he used it a couple of more times too."

"The instructions on getting rid of the body, how detailed were they? Could you tell us what they were?" Amanda let Jade do all the questioning as she was getting answers, and she felt two people interrogating might upset the rhythm.

He explained that the instructions he had been given were to take the body to the smelting works and put it in the furnace. David knew the area near the building, but also was aware they had major night security there. Jade, unaware of this, asked how he had achieved this. He said he had been told that one of the night guards went to sleep in the office and was never on duty and he should do it when that guy was working, which was every Tuesday to Friday evening, but his kidnapper had told him not to do it on the Friday. No reason was given for this. He explained that he had driven his car right up to the door, gone in and got one of the trolleys they used for moving heavy objects. He had put the body on that and wheeled it in, then using the heat resistant gloves that were always left beside the door, he had opened the door and simply put the body in the furnace. He then closed the door and left. It was very simple he said, and everything worked exactly the way he had been told.

David doubted it was that easy to do all this at such a security conscious place, but it was something that needed checked out.
When they did go to the smelting works to verify the story, they were astonished to find it was true; the guard did go into the office to sleep, there was a trolley near the door and gloves near the furnace. They were able to drive up to the building, walk-in and go right to the furnace without anyone stopping them.

When they left they went straight to David's station to say what they had done, and asked if a report of intruders came in for the warehouse on Sycamore Street to let them know, but none ever did. His story checked out, but it still wasn't proof enough. This was something he could have found out for himself, and it wasn't evidence that he had been kidnapped and given this information by someone else.
However, if it was true, the kidnapper was going to a lot of trouble to find ways for his victim to get rid of the body. Why? No one was able to identify him, so it wasn't to keep his identity secret. Was it only to stop the authorities finding out what he was doing so he could continue unhindered for longer? Or was there some other reason, and what was it?

When they met up after the interrogation the first thing Michael said to Jade was, "That Detective Hardwick...", But Jade cut him off.

"That isn't related to this case Michael, so let's concentrate on this and we will discuss that later." She looked daggers at Michael because she was reluctant to have the whole thing came out in front of the other policeman. Michael got the message and dropped the subject.

Once they were alone Jade and Michael had a conversation about what the latest victim had said. They both knew he was talking about their boss when he talked about the incompetent policeman. No two officers had the same name. What they didn't understand was how he been promoted after bungling an investigation to that extent, but it was something they wanted to find out.

Amanda, who had been present without participating until now, reminded Jade that her own boss was willing to help and maybe she should speak to him. Jade said that was something she had already had in mind to do. I also want to talk to Mr Brothers to find out if he had a case bungled by Detective Hardwick, or any detective, Jade said.

She called John and told him she needed to speak to him on a matter possibly unrelated to this case, but which was very important, and for now secret. He told her he would make himself available whenever she wanted, and she explained that she and Amanda would be there the next day. She then spoke to Brendan, telling him they had got some interesting information from the latest victim which needed further investigation and she didn't want to discuss it until she had some more answers. Brendan, as she had known he would, except this without question.

So it was that they set off for Amanda's station the following day, just the two of them. They had initially agreed that to save time, Amanda would ask Mr Brothers if he had any dealings with Detective Hardwick or another policeman while Jade had a private talk with

John. However during the journey Amanda said she had been thinking about it and didn't think this was a good idea. She felt they both needed to be there to interrogate victim 1 in case he did have useful information.

Jade went into John's office and told him all about what the latest victim had claimed. While this conversation was taking place Amanda went to her desk to check police records to see if the information was true or not. She found nothing, and at that point she knew they should have done this check before going to see John. Benedict's partner had been transferred to a remote place and demoted. It was as if he was responsible for everything that happened, not the chief constable.

It made no sense that the victim would make that up; after all it wasn't part of his excuse for killing the man he admitted to killing.

John was shocked by what Jade had told him, but when Amanda came in to say there was no information like that in the police records, although Benedict Hardwick had dealt with the case, it was John who suggested they needed to get the court records.

"I hate to say it, but police records can be doctored one way or another, but court records are not so easy to get at. Like in any profession, there are some bad policemen after all."

Jade phoned Michael and told him to look at the court records for that case to verify if the information was true or not. In the meantime, they would go and talk to Mr Brothers. Hopefully by that time Michael would have an answer for them.

Confessions of a Madman continues

If you enjoyed this, continue the story in books 3 and 4.

Follow Jade and Amanda as they struggle to find clues about this terrible crime. Some clues, naturally lead to nothing, but then, after hours of following dead ends, they get a break and things start to make sense.

Amanda and Jade interrogate one of the so-called madmen, who seems to be quite sane, providing he is telling the truth. The two officers believe he is.

One thing leads to another until they set a trap for the criminal. This does not go the way it should, but something they learn along the way helps in a totally different direction and makes their lives much easier.

Eventually all the pieces start to fall into place, but there is one thing they can't get a handle on, no matter which way they look at it. That is how the criminal chose his victims. They appear random and unconnected

There are many other books also by the same author, if you liked this one.

These are available on all Amazon sites.

www.ingramcontent.com/pod-product-compliance
Lightning Source LLC
LaVergne TN
LVHW050347160826
845677LV00014B/3837

* 9 7 9 8 8 3 8 9 3 4 2 5 3 *